First published 2002 by Walker Books Ltd, 87 Vauxhall Walk, London SE11 5HJ

2 4 6 8 10 9 7 5 3

This book has been typeset in Dickens

Printed in Hong Kong

For each other – V. S. & J.S.

Text 2002

Viviane Schwarz

Illustrations 2002

Joel Stewart

British Library Cataloguing in Publication Data:

a catalogue record for this book is

available from the British Library

ISBN 0-7445-8138-9

The Adventures of a Nose

Viviane Schwarz

Joel Stewart

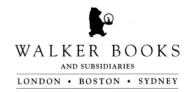

WALKER BOOKS
AND SUBSIDIARIES
LONDON • BOSTON • SYDNEY

T his is the
Nose, thinking:
"Somewhere in the
world must be a place just for me.
A place where I can fit in, and stick out.

I could be really happy there!"

He goes to the city.
Everything is big
and smells exciting.
The Nose sniffs
up and down the
streets until he is
completely lost.
"You look confused,"
calls a cat from
the city library.
"Come in here!
Here you can find things out,"
says the library cat.

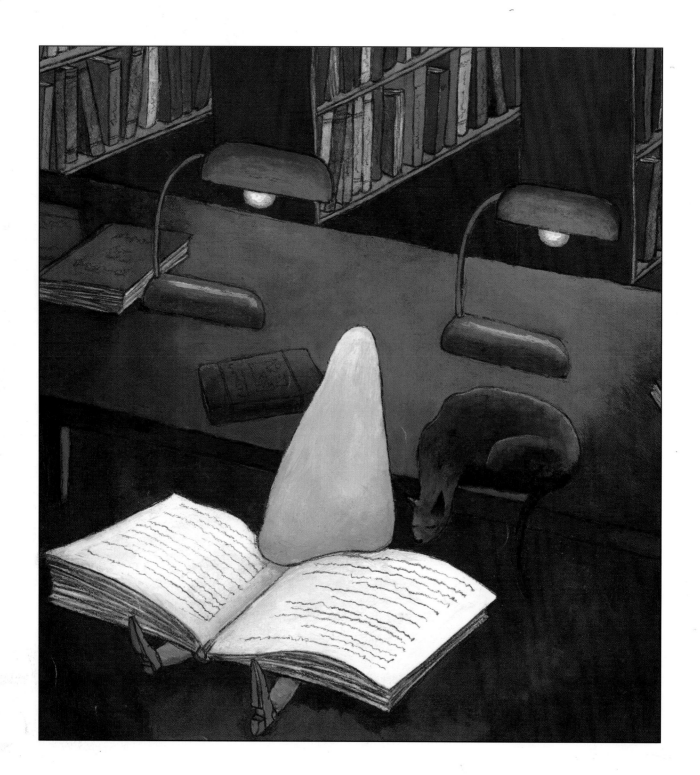

The Nose likes books.
"This one smells of ink, and
this one smells of dust," he thinks.
"Hmm. Maybe
I could stay here."
But he can't.
The library closes at night,
and everyone has to leave.
Where now?
"I know the best place
in the world," says a dog.
"Come with me!"

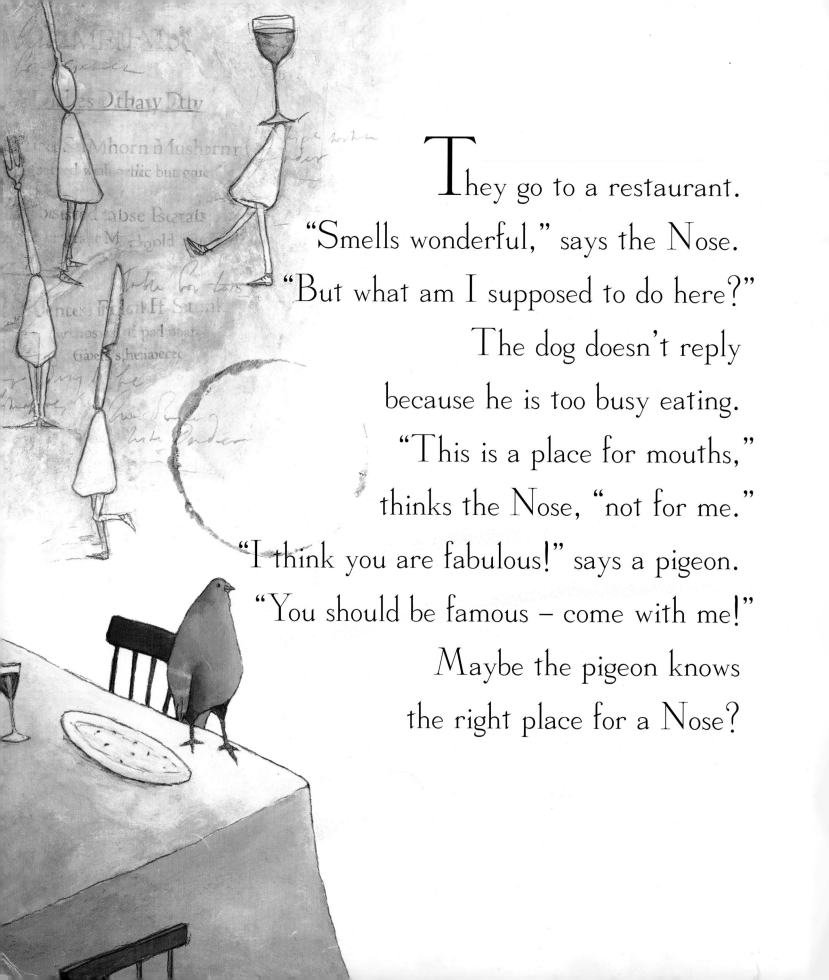

They go to a restaurant.
"Smells wonderful," says the Nose.
"But what am I supposed to do here?"
The dog doesn't reply
because he is too busy eating.
"This is a place for mouths,"
thinks the Nose, "not for me."
"I think you are fabulous!" says a pigeon.
"You should be famous – come with me!"
Maybe the pigeon knows
the right place for a Nose?

This is the Pigeon Theatre.
The Nose is doing a beautiful sneezing dance.
The pigeons cry "Bravo!"
"They are all looking at me," worries the Nose.
"It makes me feel like there is something
nasty sticking to me."
So he sneaks out and runs away,
out of the city.

This is the Nose feeling much better.
"The world is big," he thinks.
"There must be a place for me
somewhere. I will find it for myself."

The Nose climbs up,
high as the mountains
and the birds and the clouds.

He dives down,
deep as the fish
and the lowest
valleys of the sea.

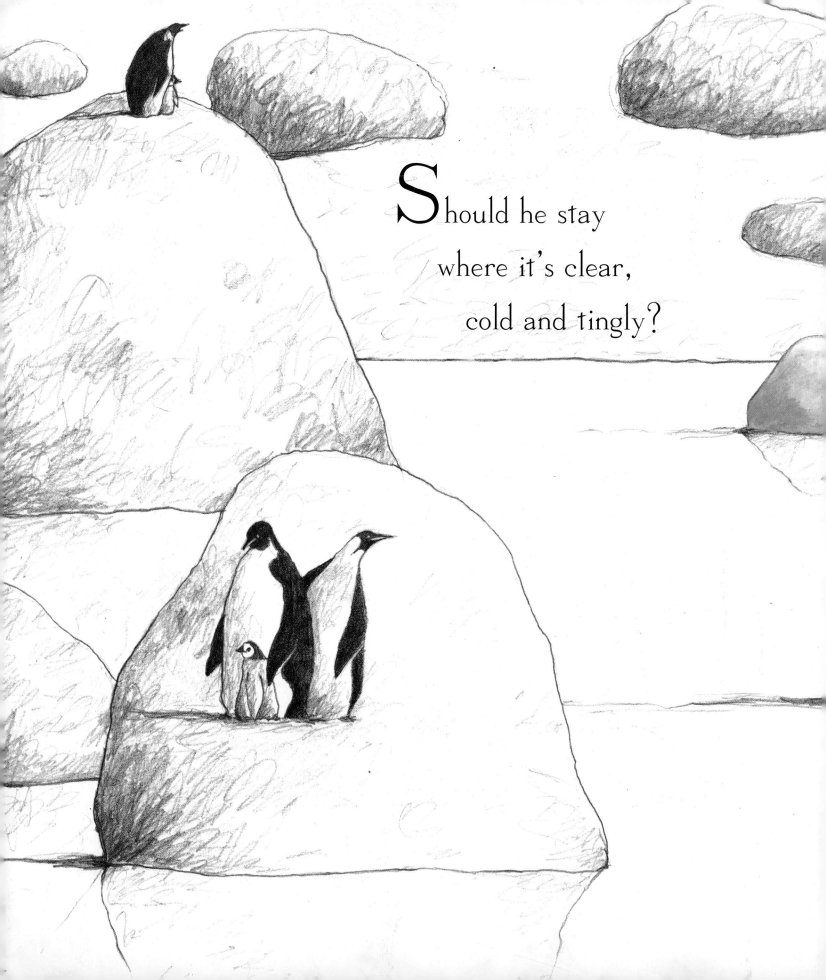

Should he stay
where it's clear,
cold and tingly?

Should he stay where it's spicy and hot?

This is the Nose feeling much worse.
He has travelled all around the world.
He has smelled amazing things.
"But I still haven't found my place,"
he thinks. "A place to fit in and stick out.
A place to be really happy.
Maybe there's something
wrong with me."

The Nose
goes to see a doctor.
"I just don't fit in anywhere,"
the Nose sniffles.
"Oh, I think you do!" the doctor says.
"Don't you see, the whole world fits
perfectly around YOU.
Your place is always in
the middle sticking out –
because you are a Nose!"

This is the Nose who has
smelled the whole world
and has found his place in it –
he fits in by sticking out, always.
"Of course!" he thinks.
"How wonderful!"